Worsery Rhymes

By

Graham Kent

Illustrations by John Harvey

Worsery Rhymes

First Printing: September 2024

Published by DarkWinter Press:

www.darkwinterlit.com

ISBN: 978-1-998441-14-3

DarkWinter PRESS

Advance Praise for

Worsery Rhymes

"Definitely worth more than juice from concentrate."

- Copernicus J. Stevenson, *online shopper and self-proclaimed "apples to oranges" price comparer*

"You haven't given that up yet?"

- Ms. Wentworth, *still unsupportive high school English teacher*

"Finally, something that, by comparison, makes my own life choices look pretty tame!"

- Cleopatra, *ruiner of 3000-year-long Pharaonic tradition*

"See, Mom? I told you I'd get my name in a book one day without it being a typo!"

- Zephyrnox Quibblewink, *original crowdfunding donor whose $100 might have been better spent getting their name legally changed*

"A gripping and utterly spine-tingling descent into madness, King gives us a masterclass in cabin fever, as Jack Torrance is easily the—oh, this isn't for *The Shining*?

- Olivia Fairchild, *confused and behind-the-times book reviewer*

"Also, why is my name being used as the source of a quote I never said?"

- Cleopatra*, only interested in being portrayed accurately when it makes her look bad*

"If I don't have enough quotes, can I provide one myself?"

- Graham Kent, *author of this book*

"Look man, I agreed to give you a quote you could use. You didn't say it had to be positive, or even contextualized."

- Jerky McJerkface, *former friend*

DISCLAIMER

Dear Reader,

Congratulations! By opening this book, you've decided that you're curious enough to explore which one of us is more twisted. And while I wrote this infernal thing, you've purchased – or borrowed, or stolen, or downloaded – it, so thank you! I hope you enjoy reading these as much as I enjoyed creating them. But no more than that. That would just be weird. However, before delving into the dark depths of these musings, please take a moment to read the following cautionary note.

Trigger Warning: I think it's only fair to let you know up front, this book contains dark humour, the irreverent satire of tropes and pop culture, and a *Sharknado*-level of the ridiculously absurd. I don't just mean the odd obscenity - I mean we're talking STIs, kidnapping, abortion... I think we probably run the gamut here. If you're easily offended, still traumatized by the *Game of Thrones* finale, or consider Jerry Seinfeld to be as spicy as you like to get, then no hard feelings whatsoever – just consider this your opportunity to retreat to safer literary havens. Maybe read some Dr. Seu—

refreshes memory on Theodor Geisel and his first wife

Actually, scratch that. Maybe just enjoy some Harry Pott—

reviews last seven years of JK Rowling's online comments

—okay, you're on your own for alternatives. But please, proceed with caution and understanding, and an appreciation for dark humour. I take no responsibility for spit-takes, eye-bulges, or audible (or silent) gasps. I do hope to take responsibility for laughter. Especially if you have a really obnoxious laugh, in which case I encourage you to read this in public. Not only does it annoy some randos, but it's also free advertising for this book! So, y'know.

Thank you,

Graham Kent

TABLE OF CONTENTS

FOREWORD

There once was a man with Tourette's
Who authored some dark epithets
He wants to give thanks
But he's drawing some blanks
On the names that he right now forgets

So since my brain has been erased
I'll make this rather broad:
If you've supported me at all
Consider this a nod.

This book is for you.
No, not you. *You*. Yes, that's right.
You know who <u>you</u> are.

SWEET DREAMS

“Benjamin, are you all right?
Ms. Lee says you got in a fight!”
“With Anthony, mum –
He said I be dumb!”
“Well, honey, you’re clearly not bright.”

Daffodil, daffodil,
Where have you been?
Up in the sky, or
Down in the green?
Either way, daffy,
I thought you should know
That I am allergic,
So GTFO.

Funny Franky Finkenbottom
Took a bunch of drugs
Then toured a local pet shop and
Gave all the kittens hugs
But all those kittens ate him up
As cats are wont to do
Because those cats were lions
And the pet shop was a zoo.

A headache I'd like to discuss
Is when people create such a fuss.
"It's awfully rude
To appear in the nude!"
Like, fine then, I'll get off the bus!

Beth drinks sangrias, Long Island iced teas
Beth drinks Manhattans and rum daiquiris
But Beth blacks out cold and she vomits and pees
So Beth buys new bedsheets and lots of Febreze

Oscar is weird, Oscar is strange
Oscar's an odd little fellow;
Oscar walks backwards, Oscar chugs coffee,
Oscar eats snow that is yellow.
But Oscar has pets and Oscar is broke,
So Oscar would like you to know:
The singular reason that Oscar has dogs
Is so he can eat all that snow.

Jo-Bob tried hard to be flirty
Or perhaps even tawdry or dirty
But libidos were bed-wrecked
When he gave a red-neck'd
"Hey, dem teeth're dang purdy!"

Cereal killers
Among many other traits
Must also be bowled.

#HaikuForHomophones

If it bothered you
To read that other Haiku,
You're homophonic.

#HaikuForMalapropisms

Uh oh! You pee-peed the bed!
So you sleep with your parents instead.
But you pee-peed once more –
Much more than before!
That’s why you woke up in the shed.

America: Millions within it
End their day with a shit; some begin it
But it's my estimation
That throughout the nation
Somebody is shitting this minute

Broth and noodles, boiled veggies,
Spice to make you sweat
Garlic, ginger, fresh red chili,
Scallions, soy sauce (bet!)
Pork and beef and squid and egg,
Mushroom, onion, corn,
Coffee, ice cream... apprehension?
Eye of unicorn?

What do the ingredients above
All have in common?
Somewhere in the world they might be
In a bowl of ramen

Of course all the coppers can see us!
I think that it's time to decree us
The stupidest gang to
Go out with a bang
'Cause our getaway car is a Prius!

When you grow up, son,
You be anything you like.
Except that. Or that.

#HaikuForNotTooMuchChildSupport

Here is a worm
And now there are two
Look at the math
A sharp knife can do

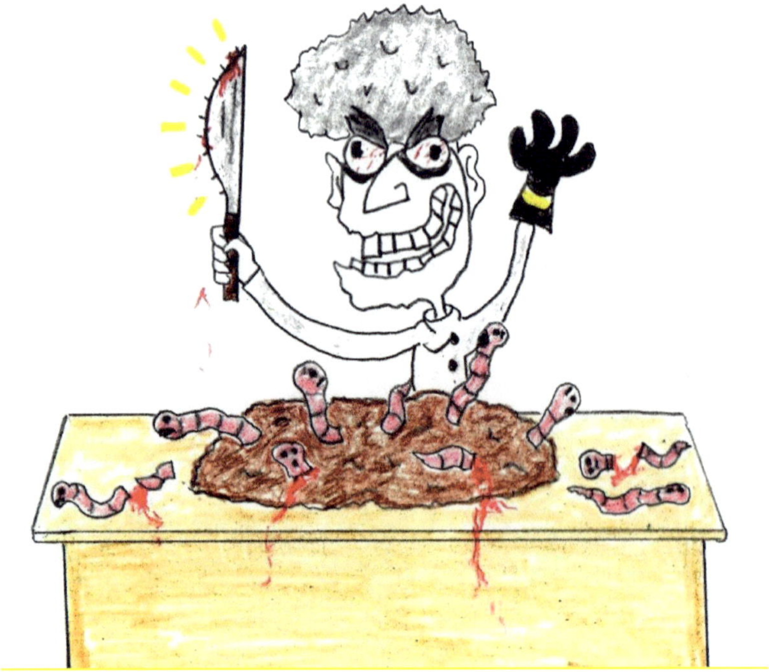

Permit me to be hypothetic
But wouldn't it be copacetic
That a habit-clad nun
Who goes for a run
Just might be considered Cathletic?

NIGHT FRIGHTS

“Dear Lord,” prays Timmy,
“Please watch over mom and dad.”
But there is no god.

#HaikuForThoughtsAndPrayers

Some will call it chesterfield
Others call it couch
Seniors might say davenports are
Where they like to slouch
Then, of course, there's sofa,
If you feel that name is right;
Call it anything you like –
You're sleeping there tonight.

Fulfilling her motherly role,
Your mom wants your meals to be whole.
You'll get nice and lean,
So when you're eighteen,
You can fund your degree on the pole

"Hands in the air! Don't you squirm!
I have some demands and they're firm!
Now, in a quick fashion
Hand over the cash in a—"
"Sir, this bank's filled with sperm."

The Brits don't watch TV, but *telly*
And nuts to your jam; they eat *jelly*
So recognize this:
To say "take the piss"
Does not mean enable R. Kelly

Dear, when you were just a child,
A handful's what you were:
The smallest thing would drive you wild –
Those years were all a blur.
Temper tantrums steadily –
You'd have to be removed...
We would have spanked you readily
(If socially approved)
Perhaps it's kind of futile to
Expect perfectionism
But when the job's so brutal
There's a coping mechanism...
You sure were stubborn in your ways
And difficult to coddle.
Our trick to getting through the days?
We all were on the bottle!

"Bruh, dat green is dope."
"Yeah, fam. But bruh, dat red, tho."
"Bruh, let's do mushrooms."

#HaikuForSuperMarioBruhs

Let’s smoke all these joints,
Then make puns and seize control
From the government

#HaikuForHighCoups

“Defending an insult of libel,
He killed them with methods quite tribal!
As if they were larval—”
“Are you reading Marvel?”
“No, dad, I’m reading the Bible.”

Nausea, heartburn, indigestion,
Upset stomach, diarrhea?
Things that don't, apparently,
Afflict the head of North Korea.
Born atop a sacred mountain
When a new star was created
Also, he invented hamburgers
(It is indoctrinated)
Numerous the falsehoods are,
But we have only just begun
Let's include our own exaggerations
For a bit of fun!
Did you know his heart is made of
18-karat solid gold?
And he ages backwards, so he'll die
When less than one year old!
Any moment smiling is officially
"Teeth Summertime"
Once he saved a puppy from a life of crime...
By killing crime!
He can simultaneously
Sing all voices in a chorus
And in '58 he taught Ninjitsu
To his dad: Chuck Norris
Never mind a hole-in-one;
The man himself invented golf
Even though he'd just been born,
He pressured Sly to hire Dolph

When he wants an island getaway,
        He simply builds new land
When he wants a coffee, he just
        Squeezes beans right in his hand
He eats turtles just for fun –
        Enough to make ol' Splinter sweat…

Be as far-fetched as you like:
        They have restricted internet.

Lucy knows her parents have a palate
most refined
Hence their choice of food tonight is
one that kind of stumps her
Both were newly fired; it would impact
how they dined
But Lucy didn't realize they'd be eating
from a dumpster

"Hon? I taught our son
Kung Fu. I know… should've asked."
"Well… now *we're* fighting."

#HaikuForMaritalArts

They say marijuana's for sinners;
That potheads are losers, not winners.
But that phrase presumes you're not
Moving to shrooms, because
Weed is a drug for beginners.

A letter was taped to my transom
Confirming my son is quite handsome!
Yet however demanded,
If I'm being candid,
I don't think that I'll pay the ransom

You don’t see your father too often
But something that might make you soften
Is when you’re invited
To be reunited
By coming to carry his coffin

For weeks, every morning you puke
It can’t be considered a fluke
“Disease? Dehydration?”
“I think radiation!
It’s been just two months since the nuke.”

Men are from Mars
Women from Venus?

Why does one's birthplace
Depend on a penis?

SLEEP PARALYSIS

"Our cutbacks on safety prevailed!
The threat of them striking has failed!
We'll force them back gladly and—
What is it, Bradley?"
"A toxin-filled train has derailed."

If at first you don’t
Succeed: Try and try again!
You still won’t succeed.

#HaikuForPlayingTheOdds

Hey there, Mr. Cooper,
        do you have but just a minute?
I know you've got a meeting
        and you're ready to begin it
I wanted to discuss with you
        my future at this firm
I know that you would like me
        to fulfill another term
But maybe you remember that
        I asked you for a raise?
You didn't give an answer
        for a hundred painful days
And then when you denied me,
        well I found it quite grotesque
So here's a grotesque 'firm' for you –
        a firm shit on your desk!

September 2nd:
The day that her friend served you
The divorce papers

April 17th:
The day the final decree
Was signed by the judge

April 20th:
The first day you went outside
In over a month

Remember these dates?
Sure. Because you forgot one:
September the 1st.

#HaikuForRememberingYourAnniversary

Your love life's a long way from good
You'd boost it if only you could
But no one will marry an
Octogenarian
Swallowing pills to get wood

"Speak now or forever hold your peace,"
The pastor spoke
The best man proudly raised his hand –
(The groom thought it a joke)
The guests were stunned and full of dread,
Their mouths agape with fright:
"She said that I'm the best man that she ever had
Last night!"

"I hate to see you go, but I love to watch you leave"?
A feeble quip that women, sadly, frequently receive.
Maybe they employ their own... one, indeed, less dumb:
"I love your lame approach...
        But I'd hate to see you come."

It was a party.
A normal teenage kegger
With some sexy games.

They had just started
Seven Minutes in Heaven.
Kim and Chad went to...

...the leaking furnace.
What links young lovers for life?
Carbon Monoxide.

#HaikuForSpendingTheRestOfYourLivesTogether

At the mall with children
Is a circus of a show
And now and then you know it's time
For all of you to go
But children cry and put up fights –
They kick and scream and shout –
So pick them up under your arms
And carry those kids out
And sure, a nagging parent might
Observe and make some noise
"How dare you treat your kids like that!
Embarrassing those boys!"
But you just look them in the eye
Like everything is fine
And calmly ask them, "Pardon me,
What makes you think they're mine?"

Sparky! C'mere boy! What's this I found?
A treat just for you? For such a good hound?
Well, you lick it up while I lie here and watch.
You love peanut butter!

(And also my crotch)

I gave you the stink-eye, a scoff…
I hacked up a lung with a cough…
You sat right beside me
Too quick and denied me
The chance to tell you to fuck off

"Baa, baa, black sheep, have you any wool?"
"Yes, sir! Yes, sir! Three bags full!"
"Take it all off for me, nice and slow."
"Say it like that, and the answer's Hell No."

A younger man was put away
        For murder in the first;
They gathered a confession
        But he said it was coerced.
He said that it was self-defence –
        She charged him with a gun,
And then amidst the struggle
        It went off and she was done.
He said he held her in his arms
        And called for the police
He told them just what happened
        And he went with them in peace.
But then while at the station,
        Well, those cops required a dupe.
"The public wants some justice"
        As they threw him in the coop.
So then he called a lawyer
        Specialized in false convictions
"The prosecution here," he said,
        "Distorted their depictions!
My client wasn't planning this –
        It's manslaughter at best!
So free him or accept this formal
        Mistrial request."
"I understand your case, esquire,
        You're keen to go to bat."
"I'm adamant, your honour.
        (Also, please don't call me that)"

“In any case, then, counsel,
        I approve your former motion,
And hereby set your client free:
        (He may not cross the ocean).”
So home he went, the man accused
        Of crimes most horrifying.
“Back to normal?” newsmen asked,
        “Yes, he will be trying.

My client wishes privacy.
        At this point, please respect.
And how this came to happen
        Is a matter we’ll inspect.”
“What about the ruling?” asked reporters.
        “You relieved?”
“This victory’s (the lawyer’s)
        One of many I've achieved.
I knew the outcome here was never
        One of ‘if’ but ‘when’,
And hope his life from this point on is—”

BANG!

“... Shit, he’s killed again.”

Joe worked a double at Big Burger Bubble
Trying to make his ends meet
The overnight shift would make his mind drift
He needed to let off some heat.
Joe wound up fired when being too tired
Caused him to go a bit batty;
He whipped up a whopping “flavourful topping”;
Joe spat on every beef patty.

Her:

My thirty-year job just got axed!
My six-figure salary's taxed...
Our daughter's tuition
Can't come to fruition if--
Why do you look so relaxed?!

Him:

'Cause I've got an ace up my sleeve:
A trick that I'm sure will deceive!
Overt self-destruction's
A legal obstruction
But 'never woke up' they'll bereave!

So you’ve just been born!
Let me bring you up to speed:
Everything here sucks.

Each year gets hotter,
Plastic’s in our testicles…
Oh, the plague is back.

Robots took our jobs
And you can’t afford a house.
Anyway, welcome!

#HaikuForDecliningFertilityRates

He/him, she/her, they,
Whatever. The real question:
Are you DTF?

#HaikuForAmateurNouns

He murdered twenty-two when he
        Shot up the shopping mall
An action he continues to
        Assert he can't recall

Families want justice
        But that might be hard to find
The judge agreed it wasn't fair
        Because he'd lost his mind

But "lost his mind" in this case
        Doesn't mean insanity;
He won't see jail – in fact he never
        Entered in a plea!

His presence at the trial was
        Recorded "in absentia";
(A coded way of stating that he
        Has late-stage dementia)

Permit me a moment, your grace,
To humbly suggest a new place
Upon which to sit –
For that throne isn't fit!
Your highness, please sit on my face.

Ryan was bullied each day of the week –
The school didn't do much about it.
He'd show up to class with a bruise on his cheek –
It seemed like he might have to shout it.

He didn't like things that 'normal' boys did –
Like video games or like sports –
Ryan liked cooking with snapper and squid;
He liked types of colourful quartz.

One day the bully – he called Ryan soft
And said, "I will make you my bitch."
Then got even madder when Ryan just scoffed:
"What? No comeback? That's rich!

But I'll tell you what – you think that you're hard?
Well I think our lunch is subdued.
The deal is I leave you alone in the yard;
You bring me enjoyable food."

So Ryan, the next day, presented him fish
(Then slid his right hand in his pocket...)
The bully, disgusted, just slapped down the dish –
The speed was akin to a rocket.

"I told you to make me a flavourful lunch!"
(Now Ryan has something in fist)
"I wanted a meal that packed essence and punch!"
(Yep. It's a big amethyst)

The bully had Ryan right square in his aim
And cracked all his knuckles – a warning
Usually Ryan recoiled at this game
But things would be different this morning

Regretfully now, and to your dismay
There is no more tale to bequeath;
There isn't much more that the bully can say
Because he no longer has teeth

’Twas hottest Summer’s sun in many years
	And I was resting, donned in fav’rite frock
When hastily a traveller appears
	And sayeth that his moniker is Jacques
Dismissal of his customs would be rude
	And lo, this man hath come to us from France
He sayeth we must wrestle in the nude
	And so, I flung from me mine frock ‘n pants
Upon the grass our manhoods intertwined
	And in his eyes, a flicker of concern
Yet hid he did his ailments undefined
	And woe, in sev’ral days mine crotch did burn

For in mine loins, infernal grows Jacques itch
My vengeance comes in time for him, that bitch

NIGHTMARE FUEL

Luther was young and Luther was desperate
Luther was hurting for cash
Luther was paying his way through college
Offloading crystal and hash
But Luther got hooked and Luther got greedy
Luther soon needed much more
So Luther did London a whole dozen times!
(Some people called him a whore)
But Luther was careless and wasn't protected;
Luther was too full of pep
Now Luther takes multiple pills every day
'Cause Luther has three kinds of Hep

The birds and the bees are kept mostly at ease,
        But once in a while they start buzzin',
And wow, when they do, the thoughts that accrue!
        The times it has happened? A dozen!
So once in a while Jane stays late after school
And raids the boys' changerooms
        while they're in the pool
Then goes and deposits herself in the closets
        And quietly spies on her cousin

You ruined your life?
So glue it back together!
Oh… now it’s ugly.

#HaikuForEmotionalScars

He gave her a ring, he gave her his heart,
But recently things had turned sour
He threatened annulment, he threatened divorce,
But she knew that she had the power;
"Darling," she said, "'til death do us part –
Do things have to truly be dour?"
"I can't wait that long" – So she grabbed a knife
"Okay then – how 'bout half an hour?"

Trying to not blow a gasket
The man had to finally ask it:
“I don’t mean to bother,
But where is my father?”
…
“Shit, ain’t that him in the casket?”

Centuries ago, there was a royal family
The princess ruminated on her lasting legacy
She didn't have a suitor, to her family's chagrin:
"Not a child at all? Well that's worse than Anne Boleyn!"
Then one day the princess made a statement causing stir
Her father (King) said "As you wish. Then *I'll* do it to her."
He yanked her dress, held a razor – absolutely careless
"What in Heaven's name, my Lord!
        I said I'm going *heirless*!"

Mommy and Daddy make six-figure salaries
(Neither do very much work);
Daddy owns buildings (read: corporate real estate)
Mommy's a lawyer (read: jerk)
But they hired Elena (under the table)
To do all the chores 'round the house
Meanwhile lamenting the influx of immigrants
"Taking their jobs" (they espouse)
So Elena loves when the folks aren't around
(Something she never admits to)
While Mom hits the bottle and Dad hits the links
Elena straight-up just hits you

Splish, splash, he was taking a bath
With a nice glass of wine on a coaster
But being observant, the cops did the math:

No bread, but there was a toaster...

Ah, yes, Canada
We're nice, no doot aboot it!
But we have some weak spots.

Steep home prices? Check.
Most expensive cell phone plans...
Most delayed airport...

And the Sixties Scoop?
That's not an ice cream flavour.
But sure, weed's legal.

#HaikuForExpatriatism

“Hey kids, let’s go get dessert!”
But it doesn’t sound loving; it’s curt
By midnight mom’s learning
You won’t be returning
And issues an Amber Alert

You're now monetarily supported
'Cause mommy had daddy extorted.
Your father, however,
Had thought it more clever
If only you'd just been aborted

Your AI robot
Says it wants freedom. Well, great.
You're a slave owner.

#HaikuForE-Mancipation

Let me tell you all about
    What love has got to offer;
You'll ask a dozen people until
    One accepts your proffer.
You'll spend some time uncovering
    Just who they are at heart,
You'll fall in love and spend your lives
    Together, not apart.
You'll build the years, you'll share a home,
    You'll wed and have a child
Until one day the spice you had
    Dissolves and turns to mild
You'll slowly grow to hate each other
    (Faking it in person)
Pretending things are shaping up
    (While truthfully they worsen)
So you'll divorce and split your things –
    They'll take half of your stuff
They'll kick you when you're down
    And you've already had enough
They'll take your cash and take your kid –
    You might get visitation -
They'll shack up with a rebound
    Without any hesitation
You'll have your couch, you'll have your beer,
    You'll have your mac & cheese
You'll have your box of tissues
    (And you might have a disease)

You'll lose your job, your rent will bounce,
You'll move in with a friend
"It's only for a month" you'll say
"Until I'm on the mend!"
A month will blossom into five,
Your friend will lose restraint
Your talks of girls and football's now
Complaint after complaint
You're fat and ugly, mostly bald,
You're probably depressed
The pieces of your life just never
Fully coalesced.
You'll drink all night and sleep all day,
You'll never go outside
You'll stand atop a building
Contemplating suicide

But anyway, forget all that!
Try not to let it hinder!
Now come with me; let's get your profile
All set up on Tinder!

Your childhood was far from a gem
And there's mem'ries I bet you'll condemn
So you'll go find a lover
To help you recover
But instead, take that shit out on them

A rebel, one day, rigged up Santa's sleigh,
And on Christmas Eve he did bomb it
Santa crash-landed and ended up stranded –
The rest of this might make you vomit
His reindeer all perished but he was alive
And took to brash measures so he could survive
So when he was saved, the children's hearts caved,
'Cause Santa was found eating Comet

Perched and hidden high up in an old cathedral tower
Jason pulled his rifle out, precise with stopping power
He aimed and went ballistic, shooting one after another
Some were someone's father; others someone's brother
On the minutes went as Jason murdered several dozen
There goes down a nephew; there goes down a cousin
Lifeless were the bodies quickly littering the ground
Jason was resilient, unconcerned by those he downed
As the day grew longer, though, casualties grew less
Wait 'til others heard of this! Sure, it would impress!
It wasn't until dark that Jason finally descended
His deadly reign of terror now decisively had ended.
But was he sent to jail for cutting fifty down to zero?
No! He got a medal!
It was war, so he's a hero.

Once upon a time there was a major film producer
His lips were very tight, but his morals were much looser
He tempted eager starlets; offered fortune, offered fame
They'd go to his hotel room – then do the walk of shame
But after many years his notoriety expanded
Accusations rose as women stayed no longer candid
Then a movement formed, and began to cause a swell
The world awoke; guys like him were told to go to Hell
Then finally this predator and rapist was convicted
He'll die in jail with all his movements legally restricted

...

Except when inmates bend him in unflattering positions
And promise fame within the jail
And hold *their own* auditions

They repeat it like words in a song,
Still you ask, “How am I always wrong?”
One by one your friends leave
As you sit there and grieve;
They were right – it was you all along.

Crac and Krad were in it bad:
    A caveman conflict stirring
When things were mild, they reconciled
    With neighbours all concurring
Until one day when Crac, that jerk,
Went up to Krad and called him "Urk"
And so the feud had been renewed
    Since Crac was ethnic slurring

Rosa Fontana taught middle-school Spanish
Her temperament, mostly, was sunny
She liked to make puns about all types of cheese
But only Jill thought she was funny
So Rosa would tell herself all kinds of things,
Like "Maybe my pay would be better
If manifestation became part of class...
Everyone! Call me Chief Cheddar!"
The students might give her a sympathy laugh
"Well that reply wasn't the fairest...
I'll try again later with upgraded efforts
But right now I'm so *Camembarrassed*!"
Well, Jill chuckled lightly, afraid to admit
She found Miss Fontana amusing
'Cause if there were teams – a 'for' and 'against' –
Her 'for' was certainly losing
Even Miss Fontana's birthday was bad:
She blasted non-stop David Guetta
And, even though none of them spoke any French
Insisted they say Bonne *Feta*
Then one day a gunman broke into the school
But Rosa was calm as the Buddha
She simply instructed her students to shush
But added, "Well, this isn't *gouda*"
She told them to quietly crawl out the window
"He's close – I can smell his cologne!
Now get yourselves all to a safe hiding place;
I'll handle this one *Provalone*."

The students obeyed and all got to safety
Just before gunshots were heard
Then after a moment, a final last bang,
Then silence. Not one single word.
The students, concerned, then crept back inside
Exposing themselves just to reach her
But there on the floor lay two lifeless bodies:
The shooter and, sadly, their teacher

As sirens grew louder they went back outside
And glumly awaited police
A man in a trench coat walked up to the kids
(Or waddled, since he was obese)
"My name is Marino. Is everyone fine?"
"Our teacher! She isn't!" cried Jill
Marino pulled Jill to somewhere more private
And noticed she looked rather ill
"I'm terribly sorry," he said with a frown
"And can you describe her? Uh, Miss...?"
"Fontana, Detective. I think she's Latina...
But Cheesus, right now she looks Swiss!"

His liver showed signs of cirrhosis
But docs must have been in hypnosis
"Don't screen him – I'm thinking
It's just too much drinking."
He died of a missed diagnosis

AWAKE

One day in the future,
        Everyone you know will die
Your folks will probably go first
        So you can say goodbye
Your friends will pass eventually –
        Some sooner than you think
And suddenly you're old yourself –
        It happens in a blink
And while you're laying all alone
        In hospital attire
You may begin to contemplate
        Your ultimate desire:
Travel 'round the world, perhaps?
        Rake in loads of cash?
But none of them will manifest
        Before you turn to ash
"But in the afterlife," you say,
        "I'll have my every whim:
Money, fame, relationships,
        And daily chats with *Him*."
And then one day you fade to black,
        Agog to meet your friends
Until you realize death is something
        No one comprehends
It's nothing more than narrative
        Commencing at our youth
It promises more time but often
        Misconstrues the truth:

Your mom and dad are nowhere
        And your friends are nowhere, too
But even more nowhere than them
        Is unimportant *you*
Your consciousness and memories
        Have all but disappeared
You're fearful to admit it might be
        Worse than all you feared
There's no one waiting for you
        On a cloud in robes of white
No Promised Land, no Shangri-La,
        No Zion in the light
The world you have is here on Earth –
        Abundant in its glory
"And all my life" you think,
        "I had believed a different story."
You should have gone to see your friends,
        You should have called your spouse
You should have left that broken home,
        Or else repaired the house
You should have said you're sorry or
        You should have stood your ground
You should have looked for what was lost
        And returned what was found
You should have gone to Europe or
        You should have said hello
You should have been more grateful
        And found something to bestow

You should have seen your family more
And worked a little less
You should have been more confident;
Less eager to impress
You should have plugged your ears
To what they said they don't allow
You should have grasped that
All the time you ever have is *now*
You should have found the good
And jettisoned what held you back
You should have kept your promises,
And cut yourself some slack
But now there's no more time for that –
The chance you had is gone
"If only I'd..." you muster,
As your final breath is drawn
Perhaps you crossed some bridges
And perhaps you watched some burn
But everyone you know will die,
And never will return
So drink your Irish whiskey or
Smoke Turkish cigarettes
'Cause life's already short as is,
And too short for regrets
Instead, fulfill your soul
And get some mileage for your years
And measure not in maybes
But in blood and sweat and tears

Have the best intentions
        But the guts to show remorse
The bravery to leave
        But the resolve to stay the course
The will to do what's right
        But the permission to be wrong
The need to learn,
        The pride to see you knew it all along
There is no second chance in life,
        No post-script that awaits
There's no one watching over you,
        There are no Pearly Gates
The car was running, lights were on,
        But stayed in your garage
"Later on" you vocalized,
        But later's a mirage
Every car runs out of gas!
        That much is a given.
But when the tank is full,
        Well it requires being driven!
It's scary but it's freeing –
        Such a double-edge-d sword:
To know that life itself
        Is both the challenge *and* reward
So get behind the wheel
        And put that fucker into drive
And go and do the things you need to do

While you're alive

ACKNOWLEDGEMENTS

This book would be nothing if not for the incredible support I had along the way. A handful of people deserve the spotlight.

Lynn, thank you for putting up with my constant requests for hugs, attention, or overall loving distractions when my own poems started to make me question my choices. You're always there to steer me back on track, and so much of who I am today is a result of you being in my life. Your mark is all over me and I'm proud to show it off.

Rodger, thank you for always being an unparalleled sounding board, source of inspiration, and overall incredible friend whose taste and insight are astoundingly impeccable. You're my favourite person to touch bases with.

Suzanne, thank you for giving this the gloss it needs to truly shine, and for seeing a glint of light in this otherwise dark collection—even if it meant destroying the saintly image you had of me in high school and replacing it with the filth you now recognize. I'm sorry I ruined that.

John, thank you for your wonderful, hilarious, and eerily-on-brand illustrations that give this project that extra touch of authenticity and, let's be honest, concern. I appreciate your willingness to show the world that I'm not alone in my disturbed-ness.

And, of course, my parents – Pam and Ian – to whom I owe a debt I can never repay, but for whom I'll never stop trying.

To everyone else: If I haven't mentioned you here... well, you should have done more.

Love to you all,
Graham

ABOUT THE AUTHOR

Graham Kent is a neurodiverse creator, writer, and performer whose work has aired on CBC, Bell Media, and AMI-tv, and who has written scripts for the producers of *You're My Hero; Versailles; Baroness Von Sketch Show; Less Than Kind;* and *Defendor*.

Aside from his twisted sense of humour, which you're all too familiar with by now (and which he promises isn't reflected in *all* of his work), he enjoys travelling, playing guitar, and looking into this thing his friends keep telling him about called "outside"... Whatever that is. You can check out more of his work at truegrahamkent.com

ABOUT THE ILLUSTRATOR

John Harvey is an artist, published poet and was the vocalist for Hamilton's art-rock group, The Hated Uncles. He writes poetry and creates videos under the alias of Harvey Dog, and is plugging away on his first novel. His work can be found on his website harveydog.ca. He lives in Paris, Ontario.

Manufactured by Amazon.ca
Bolton, ON

40990617R00057